To request permission, contact the publisher at
contactus@stearnsmg.com.

Paperback: ISBN# 978-0-9972115-4-2

First paperback edition July 2022

Written by Marnie Stearns
Edited by Holly Stearns
Cover art by Marnie Strearns & Holly Stearns
Layout by Marnie Stearns & Holly Stearns
Photograph by Holly Stearns

Printed by 48 Hours Books in the USA.

Publisher:
Stearns Publishing
4629 Roehrs Rd
Beaverton, MI 48612

Author's Website: marniestearns.com
Publisher's Website: stearnsmg.com

THE ADVENTURES OF
THE WHITE CAT

by Marnie Stearns

This book is

dedicated to

my family.

Cover Art by

Marnie Stearns and Holly Stearns

CHAPTER ONE

One day, during spring, there was a white cat, she loved winter, and summer! But she was a stray. Her collar fell off during winter and it got lost in the snow.

"Hopefully I can get picked up by someone, but there's not really a big chance," the white cat thought.

Well she was actually very wrong, because right when she thought that, a car drove to her.

"Mommy! Can I have that little kitty cat? Please?" A little boy pleaded, looking out of his window.

"Alright, fine, you can go pick him up. Or her," the mom said.

Then the little boy put the white cat in the car.

"Why am I in this giant moving box?" thought the white cat. "This boy has black hair and dark skin."

After they got home there was a dad in the house. The dad looked like the boy, but with brown hair and dark skin. The boy's sister was young, and in a princess dress. Just before that, about ten minutes ago, they were at the pet store. The white cat didn't know why, because she had thought that they had a lot of cat food at home for her already. Soon they had purchased the cat food, cat toys, and cat litter. They finally put it in the trunk of the car and went home. They were thinking of a name for the white cat, but before that they figured out she was a girl. They were thinking of names like Lily, Sweety, and other stuff like that. But then they all agreed on the name Lola. The white cat loved it!

They soon bought a collar with the name Lola on it and it said; "If found, call 555-327-6473." Lola didn't know why those numbers were there, but she kind of liked them. And when she got her new toys she was playing with them for a long time! Lola was so hungry! She wanted to try her new food, but there was a dog! The dog was eating her food? She wasn't expecting a dog eating HER food! She was furious! She hissed at the dog, but then, the humans heard her, and rushed over.

"No no Lola. Bad kitty," the boy said firmly.

Lola was scared of the dog. She needed to hide! She then ran upstairs, went under the girl's bed, and shook with her ears down. She was terrified of the big dog! Soon the little girl came up with something in her hands. Lola was shaking still, but the girl put the food under her bed that she was carrying up. Finally, Lola got to eat. She was starving, but still hiding. Hopefully that big dog couldn't find her.

"This is so good! I don't want that dog finding me though," Lola thought.

Lola started to gag.
"Hairball!" Lola thought, still gagging.

Finally, the hairball is out!
"After a lifetime, the hairball is out. Gross." Lola thought.

CHAPTER TWO

"Lola! Where are you?" the little boy shouted out.

Lola didn't want to come, but then again she would get free petting.

"Alright, I'll come," Lola said to herself.

Then she started walking out from under the bed, she saw the dog, but ignored it. Then Lola sat at the top of the stairwell like a queen on her throne. The boy was running up the stairs, but stopped on the steps while he was running. The boy picked up Lola and hugged her.

"Where am I going?" Lola thought.

The boy took Lola to his room and to his bed. Later he fell asleep.

Lola thought, "I finally got out from under the boy's arm, and I am awake as well."

"Well now that I'm out, that window is open, and I need some fresh air. I'll go get some air."

Then Lola went out the open window and sat on the roof.

"Ahh, some fresh air," Lola thought out loud. "Oh? What's that over there?"

She was curious to look at what it was. But she was out of sight from the window on the inside.

"Why is my window open?" the boy asked.

The boy had then closed his window, locking Lola out. Unfortunately, Lola didn't know this. She then saw the animal catchers.

"The animal catchers? What are they doing here at . . ." Lola checked the clock,
    ". . . 1:37 AM!"

"Yeah, they should not be here," Lola thought, unimpressed.

"There's a stray up there!" The animal catcher whispered.

"Yeah! There is one!" The other animal catcher whispered back. "Let me get it!"

"I'm tired . . ." Lola thought. "They're never gonna find me anyway."

Lola soon fell asleep, but that ended quickly when one of the animal catchers grabbed her.

"Hey!" Lola yelled. "Help!"

"Great, I'm in a van, what's worse than getting caught by the animal catchers?" Lola thought.

Lola kept hissing, and scratching the door. That made the animal catchers furious.

"Be quiet back there!" one of the animal catchers yelled.

Lola was still scratching the door of the van. "Alright! Get out!" One of the animal catchers said while getting out of the van.

The animal catchers opened the door to let Lola out. Then they took her collar off.

"What did you do that for?" Lola asked.

"Ugh, animal catchers these days," Lola thought in disgust.

Lola was walking beautifully until . . .

"CAR!" Lola exclaimed.

She ran to the side, tumbling. Lola then fainted. Later when Lola woke up, she was at the same exact place, and she was happy with that. She was happy no one cat-napped her, she was happy she slept peacefully, and she was just happy.

"Finally, that pesky dog is gone, some peace," Lola said to herself.

She then saw a huge figure. She wanted to run, but she was too tired, and she couldn't move, so she slept. After she woke up she saw a lot of figures. A whole family it looked like.

"Hello?" she asked, scared.

The two smaller figures came running up to her. They grabbed her with their dirty hands and took her outside.

"Mud bath! Mud bath!" they yelled.

The boy was a light skin with blonde hair, and the girl was a light skin with brown hair.

She saw a stray. It ran away when she looked. The kids also looked when she looked.

"Huh? What do you see, kitty? What do you see?" the boy asked.

"It's nothing!" the girl exclaimed.

The cat peeked this way again, this time I ran at it. The cat is gray with green, emerald eyes.

"Kitty!" the boy yelled.

CHAPTER THREE

"Come back here!" the white cat yelled angrily.

"No!" the strange cat yelled back. She sped up and caught the cat.

"What do you want from me?!" the strange cat yelled.

"What's your name?" the white cat asked.

"Uhh, I don't have a name. But what about you?" he asked.

"Me neither," the white cat said.

"But I thought you lived with humans!" he exclaimed.

The white cat said, "Oh them? They were mean to me, and they just adopted me! How funny is that?"

"Funny!" he said back.

"Do you wanna go find a home together?" the white cat asked.

"Of course!" he exclaimed.

The white cat went to the house she first lived in, but what she didn't know is that the people that adopted her moved away. She went to the door, jumped, and rang the doorbell.

"Woah how did you do that?" the cat asked in shock.

"Magic," the white cat replied.

The cat chuckled. A few minutes later no one answered. They fell asleep on the porch and woke up in the animal shelter.

"What?" the white cat exclaimed. "How did we get here?"

"We're trapped. . ." he said. "I was here once. I never got adopted, so I just tried running away. They got me the first few times, but the last time I tried. . . I escaped. I was trapped here for years, I was free for years, and now I'm back. Again. . ." he said. He started to cry.

"Don't cry!" The white cat exclaimed.

"I can't help it!" he exclaimed back.

"We'll find a way. I promise," the white cat said.

"Okay. . ." he said.

They heard the door open, and paused.

"Act cute," the white cat whispered.

"How?" he whispered back

"Just try!" she whispered.

They acted cute, but no one picked them up. After a few days they were hopeless. But then. . . they actually got picked up! They were shocked. As their new owner was driving them home, they looked out the window and saw a huge lake that was shiny from the sun shining on it.

"Woah look at that!" the white cat exclaimed in amazement.

"Cool!" the cat said with amazement.

When they got to their new house, it was huge! Their new owner picked them up, and went inside. Inside there was fancy cat food, fancy litter, and even fancy toys!

CHAPTER FOUR
THE BOY'S (BRIAN) POV

"Good morning mom and sis," I said to my mom and sister.

"Good morning buddy," my mom said.

"Good morning bro!" my sister exclaimed while running up to me.

My sister gave me a hug. She has light skin, brown straight hair, and freckles, like me, but I don't have freckles. I love my sister's hugs. They're the best! After my sister hugged me my mom hugged me as well. My mom is just like my sister, but with wavy hair. After my mom hugged me I was holding out my arms for one last hug, from my dad. My dad had blonde straight hair, with light skin, and freckles.

"Oh honey . . ." my mom said sadly.

She hugged me again and I thought it was my dad hugging me so I said, "I love you dad!"

"Umm bro? That's mom, and not dad," my sister said, confused.

"Huh? Oh . . . It's hard to remember

sometimes . . ." I said with my smile fading away.

"It's okay honey. I sometimes forget too . . ." mom said back.

Mom started to cry. I hugged her with all my might, then let go.

"Mom . . . I know it's been tough without dad, but you know that we still love you, right?" I asked, trying to comfort her.

"I know . . ." she replied, wiping her tears.

"Now . . . Happy New Years!" I exclaimed, trying to fix the sadness.

"You're so funny bro! It's the 31st, and not the 1st!" my sis exclaimed back.

We all started laughing. Laughing off the sadness. Soon we forgot about all of that and went on with our day.

Later, at night my mom tucked us in.

"Night mom," my sister said.

"Night honey," she replied.

"Night," I said.

"Night," mom replied.

Then we all went to sleep.

"Good morning guys! Happy New Year!" mom exclaimed.

"Happy New Year!" me and my sister exclaimed at the same time.

We went downstairs, Kylie and George meowed at us. There were delicious pancakes at the table as well. Sarah and I both said wow when we saw them. We sat at the table and ate. When I finished I told mom I was going outside to practice basketball because I was thinking of joining the team in the fall.

CHAPTER FIVE
THE GIRL'S (SARAH) POV

"Mom I'm going up to study for my math test," I say when taking the last bite of my pancakes.

"Alright sweetie. I'll see you later," mom replied.

I went to my room and got my secret pencil case for art and math. No one knows about it so I hide my pencils in it, and my secret calculator. Mom told me to give her all my calculators. I got out my secret calculator, thinking I would need it, but once I got the practice sheet out of my binder, I took a look at it.

"Wow. Unbelievable. What kind of practice test is this?" I said shocked.

"I wish these tests were harder," I said with a mad tone.

Then I started to do my test. Multiplication, division, addition, subtraction. Mostly multiplication and division.

After I finished my practice test I went downstairs to show mom. I was walking down to be greeted by Kylie and George.

"Hi guys," I said, greeting them back.

I started walking past my mom's bedroom to find her sleeping. I just went back upstairs. Kylie and George started following me. I was wondering why, but it wasn't important. I saw my brother practicing his basketball outside.

"Hey Brian!" I yelled.

"What?" he yelled back.

"Don't you need to do your practice math test?" I yelled at him.

"Oh man! I forgot!" he screamed while running inside.

That was quite hilarious. To see him running inside, and to hear him running upstairs into our room. I just ignored him while I propped up my pillow, sat by it, and read. I was reading my favorite book. It's called Darkness Awaits. After reading a few pages, I looked over, and my brother was gone!

"He must have gone downstairs," I thought. "Whatever."

I continued to read. Until I got hungry. I set my book down and started walking down the stairs. I went into the kitchen, walked to the freezer, and opened it to find my savior. Waffles. I grabbed the waffles, and got the toaster out. I plugged the toaster in and put the waffles in it. I watched them cook. I love to see them pop out. I slathered syrup onto them, went to the table, and ate.

"What's up Sarah," Brian said.

"Hi," I said with a mouth full of waffles.

"Okay?" he said.

"Waffles are good," I said.

"Hmm," he said, ignoring me.

"Did you just ignore me?" I asked.

"No," he replied.

"Yes you did!" I exclaimed.

I then covered my mouth. I realized that mom was still sleeping, and I woke her up. I decided to run upstairs. That was my best choice. I heard mom yelling at my brother for waking her up, but once he blamed me, mom said I was sleeping. He said that I yelled. So mom was coming up here to prove I was sleeping. I heard footsteps coming up and so I got scared, but then cuddled up in my covers, with the lights off of course, put on my sleep mask, and fake slept.

"See? She's sleeping!" Mom exclaimed.

"Ugh!" Brian yelled.

CHAPTER SIX
KYLIE'S POV

I am so hungry! George and I have been meowing at them to signal them, we need food. George is the cat I was chasing. I wish they could buy us a translator from cat to human.

"George, it's not worth it. We're gonna starve!" I exclaimed.

"It's okay we'll find a way," he said.

"Hm?" I asked.

"Umm I said–" George was saying.

"Not you. The humans are coming toward us," I said.

"Oh," he replied.

The human suddenly picked me up.

"Help!" I exclaimed.

"Kylie!" George exclaimed back.

We both were freaking out. Then we met. We both sat in fear with our ears down to our heads. Then we got excited when we saw . . . The pet store! I thought that we were going to get toys, but we're not in the toy aisle. It had different types of collars, normal collars, collars for cats, collars with bells, collars for dogs, and shock collars. We went past them, thankfully. I don't want to get one of THOSE. That would be a nightmare. Once we were done I was sad. I was sad because we didn't get any new toys. We had gotten something though. I couldn't tell what it was. It looked something like a collar? I don't know. I've never seen it before. I wish I knew. Now I'm mad because I don't know. George saw me being mad. I saw that he was going to say something, but then I plugged my ears so I wouldn't hear.

We got home, finally. Our owners came up to us. They put that collar on each of our necks. I don't know if I like it or not. Actually, it's fine. It's not itchy, not ugly, not fancy. It's just me. My other collar was all of those, besides ugly.

"George, do you like your collar?" I asked. "George?"

"Get it off!" George exclaimed.

"George, you don't like it?" Sarah asked. "Well you said to get it off."

"Wait. You can understand me?" George asked, in shock.

"Yeah," Sarah said.

"So can you understand me?" I asked.

"Yes," Sarah said again.

That was totally unexpected. These collars can help us speak human languages. I think it's called English. George would know. I don't feel like asking him though. I'm going to go lay on Sarah's bed.

I'm in Sarah and Brian's room, I jumped on Sarah's bed, and laid down. Then I fell asleep.

CHAPTER SEVEN
GEORGE'S POV

I don't get these collars. They translate every word you say, and it's annoying. It's annoying because if you're talking to yourself, the humans will hear you, and it's especially annoying for me. I talk to myself a lot, so they can always hear me. Also when Kylie and I talk to each other, the humans can hear us too. This collar is itchy, and ugly. Who even likes to wear black collars? Definitely not me! Black is ugly in my opinion. I'd rather have white, like Kylie has. You know what? I think I might ask her if we can switch collars. I need to find her. Where would Kylie be . . . Oh! I know just the place!

"Well she wasn't here. I really thought she would be here because of the sun, and the comfort. Sarah's bed would be the perfect place for her! Whatever. I'll find her later." I thought.

I need to sleep. I'm so tired! I went to look all over the house for a spot. I found Kylie sleeping. I smiled at that. I kept searching for a sleeping spot. Until I finally found one. Under Brian's bed. It's so warm down there. I love warm spots. I can tell Kylie does too. I bet she was lying on Sarah's bed, but then moved to the stairs. There was also still sun on the stairs too.

I can't sleep! I've been waiting for hours! 2 hours! I think I have to change my spot. But where? I couldn't find anything good around the house besides Brian's bed! Oh. I should just go to Sarah's bed. Across the room from me. I'm going under, just in case. Once I fell asleep Sarah jumped on her bed. That woke me up.

I ran onto Brian's bed and asked her, "Why did you do that?"

"Sorry George," Sarah said.

"Hmm," I said with anger.

"Whatever," Sarah replied.

She always says whatever. I can't understand why she does that. It's not nice, I don't think. Anyways I need to find a new sleeping place. I think I'll sleep on the stairs too. I would sleep in the sun, but Kylie is there and I don't want to bother her. She's just peaceful there. Kylie and I were disturbed when Sarah ran down. It woke us both up. I just told her to go back to sleep, and she did.

I was not in the mood for sleeping anymore. I was woken up by the same person, at different times, and at different places! I'm just going to play with my toys, and I'll be fine.

CHAPTER EIGHT
NARRATOR

George loved to play with his toys, Kylie loved to sleep. I, the narrator, have the power to go inside of people's heads. I'm going to see what Kylie is doing.

I have entered Kylie's head. Her head is mostly empty, but I'm going to go to her dream.

Now this is a weird dream. She's human, Sarah and Brian are her friends, George is human, and they're at a theme park on a roller coaster. I'm just a ghost cat watching her dream. If I enter her dream, I'll probably go onto the roller coaster, which is weird because I would just appear. Unless no one will see me. Because I'm a ghost cat. Let me try. Yeah, I appeared on the roller coaster. Wait . . . the power just went out, right when I got on the roller coaster. That's creepy. . . Anyway, I'm getting out of her head because she's waking up. If she wakes up her thoughts will come on, and I will be seen.

I left, and I'm invisible. I love being invisible, you can hang out by yourself, you don't get bothered, and people can go through you. Actually, I think the whole going through you part is mostly a ghost cat thing. A ghost animal can be an imaginary friend. Especially for little ones. Most of the time I don't get chosen to be an imaginary friend. It doesn't sound fun. I mean I guess I do love having kids around, but what's the point? My real name is Scribbles, but no one calls me that. I always get called a ghost cat. Yeah, only a ghost cat. Nothing else. Wait . . . What is happening?!

Where am I? A kid? I'm becoming visible!

"Hi my name is Scribbles. What about you?" I asked, kind of scared.

"I'm Russel!" Russel replied.

"That's great. Now what do you want to do?" I asked.

"I don't know Scribbles. Wanna play baseball?" Russel asked.

"Alright Kiddo," I said.

Now how do I play this?

CHAPTER NINE
KYLIE'S POV

"George guess what?" I asked.

"What," George mumbled.

"The dream I had was about us being the human kind, with Sarah and Brian there as our friends, and we were on a roller coaster. Also the power went out when we were half way through the roller coaster," I explained.

"Wait. When the power goes out in your dream, that means a ghost cat has entered it!" George exclaimed.

"What . . ." I said with fear in my voice.

I couldn't believe it. I was standing as still as a statue. I began to walk downstairs until I saw a huge cat. He or she looked like paint was splattered all over his or her face, and was gray with white stripes.

"The humans will see you!" I exclaimed.

"No no no. They're too old for me," The huge cat said calmly.

"How are they too old for you?" I asked.

"Well, I'm an imaginary friend! Now my kid Russel taught me how to play baseball," he said.

"Well. Okay, but won't the humans see you?" I asked.

"Nope," he said with no hesitation.

"Okay–" I was saying until I got cut off.

"I'm invisible right now," he said.

"Okay," I repeated.

"Oh my gosh!" George exclaimed.

"Hold on. I'm not gonna hurt you!" he exclaimed. "I'm Scribbles!"

"Won't the–" George was saying until he got cut off.

"Nope. That's because I'm invisible!" Scribbles exclaimed.

"Oh, okay," George said, calmer than me.

CHAPTER TEN
SCRIBBLE'S POV

I don't get why everyone is scared of me, besides Russel, but you know. It's just hard to be treated unfairly, not like everyone else. Anyway, I'm going to go play tag with Russel. At least he's not scared of me.

"Hey Russel!" I exclaimed.

"Hi Scribbles," Russel said.

"Wanna play tag?" I asked.

"I can't, I'm at baseball practice," Russel said.

"Oh, Okay. . . " I said.

I don't get why he plays baseball. I thought he was in kindergarten. Or maybe it's called T-ball. He's too young for this! I miss my old Russel. When will he be done? I´m just going to go back to his house. . .

"Scribbles I'm home!" Russel exclaimed.

"Russel?" I exclaimed.

"Yeah," Russel said.

"Now do you wanna play tag?" I asked.

"Definitely," Russel replied.

"3, 2, 1 . . . Go!" I exclaimed.

"Tag you're it!" Russel exclaimed.

"Scribbles runs, and he speeds up, and . . . tag you're it!" I exclaimed.

"Oh it's on!" Russel exclaimed.

That was fun, definitely. I got the gold medal for tagging the most! Well for being the fastest too, but what's important is that Russel had fun!

CHAPTER ELEVEN
SARAH'S POV

"New year, new me. So what's on the bucket list? Be able to keep my side of the room clean, dye a strand of my hair pink, and don't laugh at my brother for a week. Don't know how that will work out." I thought.

I just scribbled that out. I laugh at my brother all the time, so if I can't do it for a week, I'll be doomed.

"Hey sis. What are you doing?" Brian asked.

"Oh nothing. Just homework. Can you get out?" I asked.

"Ugh, homework is boring. I wish you were doing your bucket list to see what you wrote." Brian said, disappointed.

That was a close one, because in my family, we are not allowed to share our bucket lists with anyone. Not your family, friends, and not even pets! I don't know why we're not allowed to share it though.

"What time is it?" I thought to myself. "10:35? What!"

After I saw that I was scared my

mom would find out, and I would get grounded, and, and . . .

"Brian Sarah wake up!" mom yelled. "Breakfast is ready!"

"Coming," I said.

As I sat at the table to eat my pancakes, Brian ran like lightning out of here. I was sad it was not waffles. I just knew all we had was pancakes. While Brian's pancake had a smile, mine had a frown.

"Alright kids, time for school," mom said.

"Okay," I said.

"Okay!" Brian exclaimed, cheery.

I just know I'm going to have the worst day ever.

CHAPTER TWELVE
BRIAN'S POV

School, school, school, school. So exciting! I love all the subjects! ELA, science, social studies, and most of all, math! For a 4th grader, I'm pretty smart. Well I'd say, I'm the smartest kid in the class! My favorite part of the day is when we switch classes! It's just like high school, or so my friend Derik said. The teachers stay in the class, while we go in a single file line, to our lockers, get our stuff for the subject, and head there. It goes to ELA, then science, then social studies, and then math.

"Brian!" Derik exclaimed. "Time to switch classes!"

"I'm hurrying!" I exclaimed.

"Hurry faster!" Derik exclaimed.

"You be quiet!" I exclaimed.

I packed all my things and ran to my locker. Derik helped me get my science things. We both ran to the classroom, 2 minutes late.

"What were you kids doing?" Mrs. Dunkin exclaimed. "You are 2 minutes late!"

"Sorry Mrs. Dunkin," Derik and I said.

"That doesn't explain. What were you doing?" Mrs. Dunkin asked.

"I was trying my best," I said. "I was trying to get all my stuff in time."

"Okay. Just get to your seats," Mrs. Dunkin said.

It was school spirit day. We live in Beaverton, so Derik was wearing a hand made sweater that his grandma made. It had the Beaverton logo on it, with the name "Beaverton'' on it as well. Derik is my best friend, he's an inch taller than me, he's ginger, and he has freckles.

CHAPTER THIRTEEN
DERIK'S POV

Science sucks. It's so boring.

"Bro, wake up," Brian said.

"What?" I asked.

"Science is over," Brian said.

"Oh!" I exclaimed. "We need to go!"

We then had to start running to my locker. I'm lucky that I helped Brian, or else he wouldn't have helped me. We then started running to social studies after we got my stuff. We made it to social studies with 1 minute to spare. I'm glad I like social studies because I wouldn't be able to fall asleep during it.

"Open to page 3" Mr. Freid said.

"Page 3," I thought.

We all then flipped to page 3.

"Bro wasn't that awesome?" Brian asked.

"Yeah! Especially learning about the states," I said.

"I think I'm gonna like the countries better," Brian said.

"Yeah," I said.

"Well math is next," Brian said.

"Yep" I said.

I'm bad at math. There's a test today too. I wish I was sick today. I am nauseous.

CHAPTER FOURTEEN
SARAH'S POV

I walk into class, I see there is a test, and go to my seat. I'm tired so this is not helping. I look at my table partner, Derik, and he's sweating. This is the 3rd grade math review test, so I don't know how he's sweating. How would he have passed 3rd grade if he was sweating this bad, he just needs a review probably.

"Sarah, focus on the test. Not on Derik," I thought.

The test is over so I'm going to read Darkness Awaits. I really love this book because I'm getting to a mysterious part. Darkness Awaits is about a 12 year old girl, her name is Sarah, and she's experiencing very sad things for a 12 year old to experience, like divorce, moving, and other things. Darkness Awaits.

"Wow. That took a long time." I thought.

"Alright class, collect all your stuff!" Mrs. Harli exclaimed.

"Yes Mrs. Harli," I whispered.

"Yes Mrs Harli," my friend, Brielle said.

I giggled a little bit because Brielle must have heard me whisper it. We both quietly giggled. Everyone besides me and Brielle started running.

They were all calling, "Recess!"

Brielle and I were just talking. I then started running, and Brielle chased me all the way to the playground.

"Can't catch me!" I exclaimed.

"Oh I will!" Brielle exclaimed.

We both laughed. I fell down on the wood chips laughing. That hurt, but I was still laughing. I had wood chips in my arms. It turns out, I had the best day ever.

CHAPTER FIFTEEN
BRIELLE'S POV

"Brielle Woodchester!" Principal Lara exclaimed.

"Yes Principal Lara?" I asked.

"Come to my office this instant!" she exclaimed.

"Yes," I said.

I'm at her office. She called my parents. I don't know what I did wrong, but it's something bad. My parents are here . . .

"I witnessed Brielle bullying her best friend!" Principal Lara exclaimed.

"WHAT!" I exclaimed. "I would never! She's my best friend!"

"Brielle . . . " My mom whispered under her breath.

"She FELL over!" I exclaimed.

"Brielle!" My mom exclaimed. "Do NOT yell at Principal Lara!"

"Well, it's the truth," I said with anger in my voice.

"I'm going to get Sarah to see what she thinks about it," Principal Lara said.

"Okay," I said.

"Sarah Keil please come to my office. I repeat Sarah Keil Please come to my office," Principal Lara said.

I'm sweating. I know Sarah won't lie, but will this be the first time? I'm scared she will lie. I'll get in trouble. I'll get detention!

"Yes Principal Lara?" Sarah asked, poking her head into the room.

"Come sit," Principal Lara said. "Did Brielle bully you?"

"No of course not!" Sarah exclaimed "She's my best friend!"

I'm glad she was honest and said I didn't, she's my best friend. I'd never want to hurt or bully anyone.

CHAPTER SIXTEEN
BRIAN'S POV

"Yo what's up Derik," I said.

"Yo what's up!" Derik exclaimed.

"I've been waiting for like 2 hours," I said.

"I know, and I'm sorry I was just so busy doing homework," Derik said.

"It's fine I was doing homework too," I said.

"Yup, okay was it math, science, social studies, or ELA?" Derik asked.

"ELA and math," I said.

"Science and social studies," Derik said.

"Nice," I said.

"Nice," Derik replied.

"So what should we do?" I asked.

"Ride our bikes to the playground?" Derik asked.

"I would have to ask my mom," I said.

"Okay call me back," he said.

"Alright," I said. "Bye."

"B—" Derik started.

I accidentally hung up on him, but I didn't notice. I grabbed my book, put it in my extra backpack, and asked my mom if I could go to the playground.

"Mom, can I go to the playground?" I asked.

"Sure," mom said, "but don't be home late!"

"What time?" I asked.

"5:50," mom said.

"Okay," I said.

CHAPTER SEVENTEEN
DERIK'S POV

"Where is he?" I thought to myself. "Oh there."

"Hey," Brian said.

"Hi," I replied.

"Let's go in!" Brian exclaimed.

"Okay," I said.

"Let's go on the swings," Brian said.

"Yeah," I replied.

I left my bike by Brian's, so I wouldn't lose it. We're walking to the swings, but I like the slides better. Especially climbing up them. We're not allowed to in school, but when Brian and I ride our bikes here after school, we can do whatever we want. We're almost to the swings, so I don't want to say anything.

"Derik?" Brian asked.

"Yeah?" I asked.

"Do you want to race?" Brian asked.

"To what?" I asked.

"The swings," Brian replied.

"Yeah," I said.

"3 2 1 go!" Brian exclaimed.

"Hey! No fair you went before me!" I exclaimed back.

"You snooze, you lose!" Brian exclaimed.

"Whatever man," I said.

CHAPTER EIGHTEEN
KYLIE'S POV

I don't know where Brian went. Brian's mom said the numbers on the clock would read 550. It's 549. Oh! Now 550!

"Brian's mom!" I exclaimed.

"Yeah?" She exclaimed back.

"It's 550!" I exclaimed.

"Okay!" She exclaimed back.

It's 551! Brian's gonna be in big trouble. Brian's home. I have to tell him that he's in big trouble.

"Brian," I said.

"Yeah Kylie," Brian said.

"You're in big trouble!" I exclaimed. "It was 551 when you came home, and not 550!"

"For 1, It's 5:51 or 5:50, not 551 or 550. For 2, It's one minute late!" Brian exclaimed.

"Where is your friend you went with?" I asked.

"He's home, why?" Brian asked.

"I wanted to see him," I said.

"Well, he's not here, so better luck next time," Brian said.

That made me mad-sad. I wanted to see Brian's friend! At least I still have George.

"Where is George? I need to go looking for him," I thought.

I checked upstairs, I checked the beds, I checked the bathrooms, and I checked the library they have. George is nowhere to be found. Unless he's hiding somewhere. I'll check around the house.

CHAPTER NINETEEN
GEORGE'S POV

I am hiding in my hang out place. It's under Brian's bed, but behind some stuff. I'm going to get my needed rest, and when I wake up I'll get some food. Every time I rest, I get super hungry when I wake up. It's awful because then I'd have to leave my hang out place, get food, and come back up. It uses up my energy. Now I'm going to get my needed rest.

"George!" Kylie exclaimed. "I found you!"

"What . . ?" I asked, sleepily.

"Wake up!" Kylie exclaimed.

"Fine. . . " I said.

I got up, and came out of my hang out spot. I went to the library. I saw the book The Space Encyclopedia.

"Kylie, come look at this," I said.

"Coming," Kylie said.

"Look, The Space Encyclopedia," I said.

"Woah," Kylie said, with a sparkle

of excitement in her eyes.

"It's cool, right?" I asked.

"Yeah," Kylie said, picking up the book.

"Alright bye mom!" Sarah yelled. "I'm Going upstairs!"

"Bye hunny!" Sarah's mom yelled back.

"Hey guys," Sarah said. She then stopped running.

"You like my Encyclopedia?" Sarah asked.

"Yeah!" I exclaimed. "It's so cool!"

"I'll read it to you," Sarah said. "Scootch in."

She read it to us. It was so cool and interesting, that I couldn't fall asleep. Kylie fell asleep, but I couldn't. It was so cool!

CHAPTER TWENTY
KYLIE AND GEORGE'S POV

Kylie: "What's that sound?" I asked.

"Thunder. . . " George said.

"What's thunder. . . ?" I asked.

"Very, very, very bad. . . " George said.

The house is shaking, it's so loud, I can't take it!

George: "I can't believe it. . . " I said.

"What?" Kylie asked.

"Nothing. . . " I replied.

"Okay. . . " Kylie said.

This is crazy. I have never experienced this in a house. I've always experienced this outside, not inside. Lightning struck, and it lit up the window.

TO BE CONTINUED . . .

AUTHOR'S NOTE

A LITTLE SOMETHING ABOUT MYSELF

I am Marnie Stearns, and I'm a 10-year-old author. I started writing when I was little. I discovered my passion for writing when I was 5. I wrote many short stories, and I did my best to write as much as I could in this book. I started writing this very book in school, with the help of my ELA teacher, Ms. Schaiberger. I also want to credit my family, and grandparents for supporting me on this journey of mine.

I mostly write fiction books, but I will also write some non-fiction books too. I hope you enjoyed reading this book!

From,

Mamie
Stearns
2022